LP
2113

Peepsqueak

Wants a Friend!

Written and illustrated by Leslie Ann Clark

HARPER

An Imprint of HarperCollinsPublishers

Library of Congress Cataloging-in-Publication Data is available.
ISBN 978-0-06-207804-9

The artist used pen, then scanned and finished the art
in Adobe Illustrator and Photoshop to create
the digital illustrations for this book.
Typography by Jeanne L. Hogle
12 13 14 15 16 SCP 10 9 8 7 6 5 4 3 2 1

To all my Grand-bebes!
To Bodie and Tate and _____ ?
And as always, to my Bear, with love.

—L.C.

As the sun came up over the farm, all the baby chicks went running into the yard to play.

2 by 2! 2 by 2! 2 by 2!

Peepsqueak ran out too. Then he came to a STOP!
He was only 1.

"I need a friend!"

he called.

Peepsqueak looked around and saw everyone running in pairs.

So he hopped and skipped and ran OUT of the barnyard and into the woods in search of a friend.

Two baby chicks gasped.

"Don't go into the woods, Peepsqueak!"

Peepsqueak said, "You are 2 but I am 1;
my search for a friend has just begun."

Then Peepsqueak hopped, skipped, jumped, and skittered down the path.

There on the path were footprints—very BIG footprints!
Peepsqueak skidded to a STOP!

This could be a friend, he thought. A very, very big friend!

Then Peepsqueak
hopped, skipped, jumped,
and skittered down the path,
looking for his very, very big friend.

Along the way, Peepsqueak met up with 2 hedgehogs.
"Are these your footprints?" asked Peepsqueak.
"No," said the hedgehogs. "They're too big for us.
You'd better not go any farther," they added.

But Peepsqueak said, "You are 2 but I am 1;
my search for a friend has just begun."

Then Peepsqueak
   hopped,
      skipped, jumped,
         and **skittered** down the path.

A little while later, it began to rain. 2 red birds flying overhead called to Peepsqueak.

"It's raining, it's pouring!" they said. "You had better go home!"

"I don't mind," Peepsqueak said. "You are 2 but I am 1; my search for a friend has just begun."

Then Peepsqueak
hopped,
skipped,
jumped,
and skittered
down the path.

Down the road Peepsqueak ran, farther into the woods, jumping over puddles and skipping over holes.

2 raccoons stood under a bush, eating some apples. "It's lunchtime, Peepsqueak," they said. "You'd better go home."

Peepsqueak said, "You are 2 but I am 1;
my search for a friend has just begun."

Then Peepsqueak

hopped, skipped,

jumped, and **skittered**

down the path.

The big footprints continued through the tall trees and ended at the entrance to a dark cave. Peepsqueak peeked inside.

"Hello, friend!" he yelled.

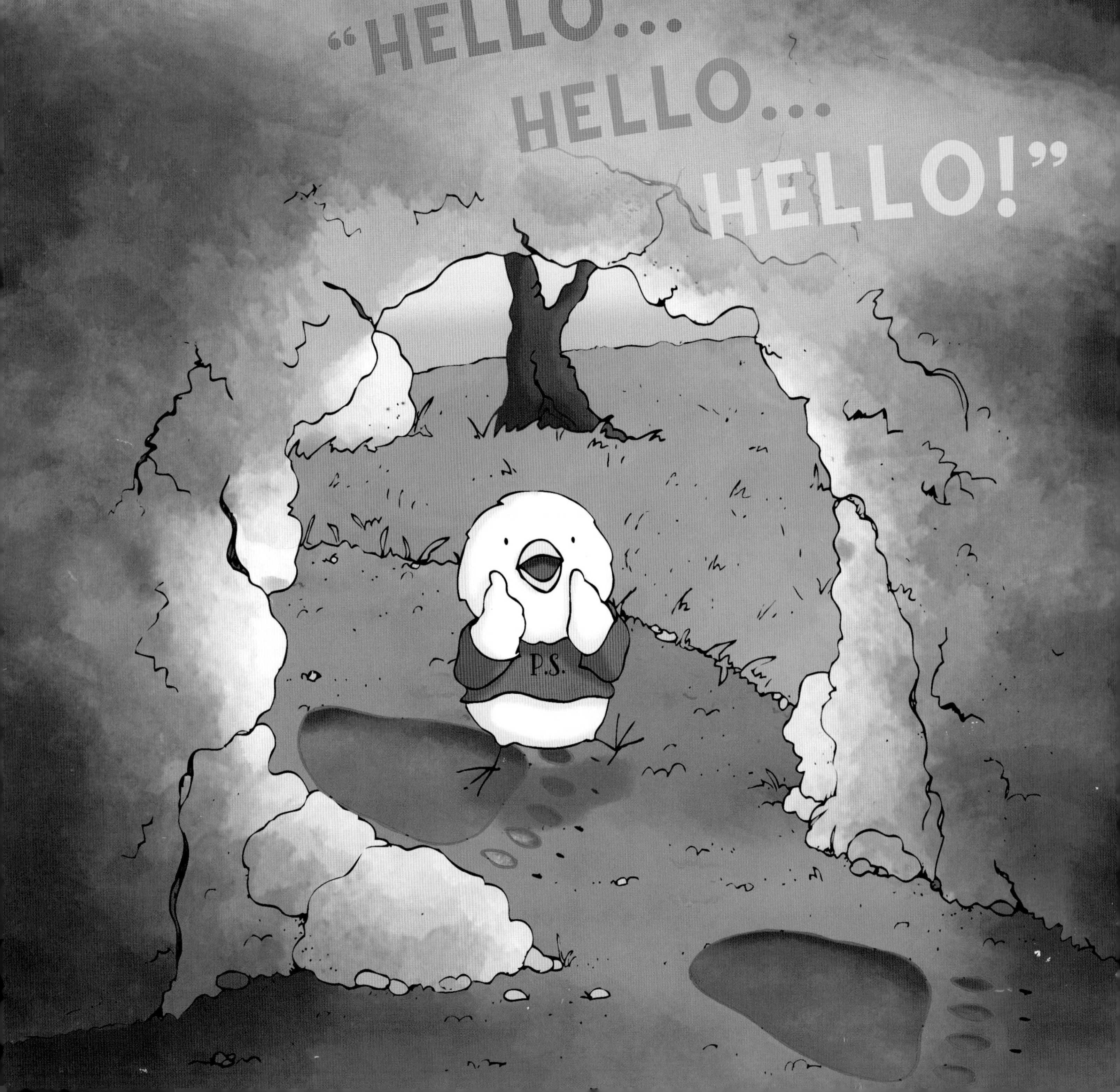

Peepsqueak paused for a moment.

Then he

hopped,
skipped,
jumped,
and skittered into the cold, dark cave.

Back at the farm the baby chicks played all day,

2 by 2,

2 by 2,

2 by 2.

Then they heard a noise coming from the woods.
It sounded like a growling noise mixed with a tiny peeping sound.

2 by 2, 2 by 2, 2 by 2,
the chicks looked at one another and gasped!

Grrrrr!!!

Peep, peep, peep!!!

Into the barnyard came Peepsqueak with his new friend . . .

A GREAT BIG BEAR!!!

All the animals scattered. But Peepsqueak and Big Bear

hopped,

skipped,

jumped,

and **skittered** around the barnyard!

Peepsqueak yelled,

"Friends don't just come in 2s.